that's SO raven

Step Up

Adapted by Alice Alfonsi
Based on the series created by
Michael Poryes
Susan Sherman
Part One is based on a teleplay by
Susan Sherman
Part Two is based on a teleplay by
Dava Savel

Watch it on
DISNEY CHANNEL abc Kids

Disney PRESS

VOLO

New York

Printed in the United States of America

First Edition
1 3 5 7 9 10 8 6 4 2

Library of Congress Control Number: 2004112617

ISBN 0-7868-4659-3

For more Disney Press fun, visit www.disneybooks.com
Visit DisneyChannel.com

Part One

Chapter One

"**O**kay," said Raven Baxter, worriedly checking her watch, "she's almost here."

Raven and Chelsea Daniels, her best friend, were sitting in the Baxters' living room. Raven plunged her hands into the shopping bag sitting on the coffee table and pulled out two pairs of brand-new shoes. "These or these?" she asked Chelsea.

Chelsea studied the red stacked sandals and fringed suede boots. Both looked totally hot. But Chelsea knew no pair of shoes was going to solve Raven's *real* problem.

"Rae," said Chelsea in a firm voice, "you always freak out every time your cousin Andrea comes in from Europe."

And do you know *why*? Raven wanted to ask her. Because the girl is untouchable! She has perfect skin, perfect hair, perfect teeth. And she buys her clothes in places like France and Italy. How can I compete with that?

But Raven wasn't about to admit any of that—not to Chelsea, not to anyone.

"Girl, I am *fine*," Raven lied with a wave of her hand. An instant later, that same hand dove back into the shopping bag and pulled out two new hats. "I just need to know which hat says, 'Thanks for coming, but you need to go back to Paris.'"

"Rae," Chelsea said with a sigh, "she's only going to be here for a little while."

"Okay, I understand that," said Raven, putting down the hats and frantically fishing around inside the bag once more. "But does this *belt* say, 'Just because we're relatives, doesn't mean I have to like you'?"

Chelsea just shook her head.

Suddenly, the front door swung open and Eddie Thomas, Raven's other best friend, rushed in. "Okay, where's Andrea?" he asked with an eager grin. "Is my little French pastry here yet?"

Raven scowled. One whiff of Parisian perfume and my boy turns into a double-crossing dog, she thought. No, make that a double-crossing French poodle.

"Eddie, how can you like her so much?" Raven snapped. "She is such a snob."

"Because she's not like other girls around here, Rae," Eddie replied. "She's lived in Rome, London, Paris . . . and she's turned me down in four different languages: *nein, nyet, non,* and the ever-popular 'ain't gonna happen.'"

"You know what?" said Raven, buckling her brand-new red belt around her new low-rider jeans. "She is so phony. I can't stand that about her."

Just then, Raven's parents and her little brother, Cory, waddled through the front door, weighed down with enough designer luggage to crush a small car.

Waltzing in behind them, swinging her matching designer handbag, was Raven's cousin, Andrea.

"Look who's here!" cried Mr. Baxter, his back bent from the weight of all the suitcases.

"Ravey!" exclaimed Andrea, rushing across the living room with a squeal of delight.

What a fake, Raven thought. Then, with a fake squeal of her own, she gushed, "Oh, hi, Andrea! My girl, what is goin' on?"

The two girls met in the middle of the living room. "Smooches!" cried Raven, and they gave each other phony air kisses.

Raven gave her cousin a quick once-over

and was sorry to see that her wardrobe looked as chic as ever. Andrea's shiny copper pants and matching top perfectly complemented her fur-lined leather coat. And her straightened hair looked sleek and glossy beneath a trendy, brimless cap. From her perfect shoes to her flawless makeup, Andrea always looked like she'd just stepped off a fashion-show runway.

Unfortunately, her supermodel look came with an attitude to match. "It's *Ahn*-drea now," Raven's cousin announced in a snobby tone.

"Oh," said Raven, though what she wanted to say was *Oh, puh-lease!*

"I changed it when we moved to Paris," Andrea continued. "We live right near the Eiffel Tower." She paused to take off her sunglasses and look down her nose at Raven. "That's the tall, pointy thing you might've seen in magazines."

Raven forced a laugh—mostly to keep

herself from forcing those trendy glasses down her stuck-up cousin's throat.

"Ooh, girl," Raven replied, "how I will miss that sense of humor when you go back. . . . *When* is that exactly?"

"In a week," said Raven's father, rushing in to defuse the potentially lethal glares the cousins were giving each other. "But until then, we're going to have a *nice* family visit. Unlike the *last* one—" he added, throwing a pointed look at Raven, "when the gum was put in the hair—"

"—after the doll was put in the toilet," added Raven's mother, throwing an equally pointed look at Andrea.

At once, both girls cried, "She started it!" Then they burst into fake laughter. Raven's mother and father just rolled their eyes. This was going to be one long week—and everybody knew it.

"So, Andrea," said Raven, after Mr. and

Mrs. Baxter had gone upstairs, "you remember Eddie and Chelsea."

Andrea aimed her plastic smile across the room and said, "So, Chelsea, Cory tells me you two are dating."

"What?" Chelsea cried, outraged. She glared down at Raven's younger brother.

"We gotta share our love, baby," said Cory. Then he pursed his lips and gave Chelsea his *call-me-Doctor-Love* look.

Chelsea fumed. Get real, she was about to tell him, you're a little kid, and you wear bunny pajamas. But Cory fled for the stairs before Chelsea could get the words out.

"Well," Andrea said, turning toward the stairs herself. "I'm going to go freshen up now. You know how tiring those long international flights can be." Pausing, she glanced back at Raven and added, "Oh, right. You don't. See you, Ravey."

"Oh, see you soon," Raven called sweetly. But as soon as her cousin disappeared, she turned to her friends. "'I'll see you, Ravey,'" she said, mimicking Andrea's stuck-up voice. Raven squeezed her eyes shut. "Oh, she gets on my nerves!" she cried in frustration. "Everything is so perfect with her. Perfect life, perfect hair, perfect shoes. And then she comes into my life, interrupts everything, and you know—"

Suddenly, Raven's head started to spin. She felt her skin begin to tingle and the world seemed to freeze in time—

Through her eye
The vision runs
Flash of future
Here it comes—

I see my kitchen at night . . . which night?
I don't know, but my super-snobby cousin is

standing by the kitchen table. As usual, she's totally stylin' in an all-white designer outfit with a matching beret on top of her sleek black hair.

Eddie's there, too, standing right in front of her. He's all puppy-eyed and practically drooling, the traitorous dog.

Yo, wait a minute . . . what's my cousin doing? She's leaning toward Eddie, taking his chin in her hand, puckering her lips, and—

No!

I am NOT seeing this! She did not—

"*Kiss* Eddie?" Raven blurted out as she shook free of her vision. Shocked, she turned to her two best friends. Chelsea looked horrified. And Eddie . . .

Raven frowned. Eddie looked like he'd just won an all-expenses-paid trip to Paris.

Chapter Two

Raven stomped into the kitchen. This discussion was about to get loud, and she didn't want anyone upstairs—namely, Andrea—to overhear it.

"You actually had a vision of Eddie kissing Andrea?" asked Chelsea, following Raven into the kitchen.

"Really?" Eddie was right behind them. "Don't you toy with me, woman."

Raven wheeled on her friend. "Eddie, how could you kiss her?" she demanded. "I mean, you know how I feel about her."

"I didn't do anything!" he protested.

"Yeah, but you're *going* to," she pointed out.

"Not if you don't want me to," said Eddie.

"I mean, c'mon, Rae, you know that we're friends."

Raven sighed. Eddie was right. She was accusing him of something he hadn't even done. On the other hand, her visions of the future always came true—although sometimes, like *now*, she wished they didn't.

"You know, Rae," said Chelsea, "if you want her out of your life, this kiss might not be a bad thing. If she's busy with Eddie all week, she won't be around to bug you."

Raven put her hands on her hips. "What kind of friend would I be if I did that to Eddie?"

"A *good* friend!" Eddie eagerly insisted. "A *best* friend! So, when do I get to kiss her?"

"Well, I don't know *when*," said Raven. "But I know you guys were standing right there." She waved her hand toward the kitchen table.

"Over there?" asked Eddie, zooming in on the exact spot.

"Right there," Raven confirmed, nodding.

Eddie rushed to the table and stood on the spot. "Right here?" he double-checked.

"Eddie, right there!" repeated Raven, exasperated.

Satisfied, Eddie struck a pose, propping his hand on his hip, half-closing his eyes, and puckering up his lips.

Raven and Chelsea stared at him. "What are you doing with your face?" Chelsea asked.

"This is my kissing face," said Eddie. Then he made it again. "Watch out now."

Chelsea shook her head. "That explains so much," she said.

Just then, Andrea came down the back stairs. "Here I am, all," she called. "Miss me?"

"I know I did," Eddie said, sidling up to her.

In that instant, Raven knew she could *not* spend an entire week in the presence of Miss Stuck-On-Herself. Chelsea's suggestion of dumping Andrea off on Eddie suddenly seemed worthy of the Nobel Peace Prize.

"You know, Andrea," said Raven, "our friend Eddie here made the basketball team this year."

Chelsea nodded. "And you know, he's also such a good rapper," she added.

Ignoring them, Andrea made a beeline for the kitchen doorway. "Oh, my goodness!" she exclaimed, pointing to the doorframe. "Look, these marks are still here, Ravey. Remember when your dad used to measure us? You'd get so angry that I was always just a *l-i-i-i-tle* bit taller than you."

Raven gritted her teeth. "I don't remember that," she said.

As the temperature in the room rose from

uncomfortably warm to volcanic, Chelsea quickly jumped between the cousins. "So . . . isn't your dad a colonel in the army?" she asked Andrea, holding off a steaming Raven.

"Yeah," said Andrea, "and we get to live all over the world and meet lots of fascinating people. But once a year I take a break from all that excitement and visit Raven."

Oh, thought Raven, so I'm a *break* from excitement. In other words, I'm a *bore*. Girl, she said to herself, you are *so* asking for it!

"Well, actually," Raven said snidely, "since you moved to Paris, it's *Rah*-ven."

Raven and Andrea burst into another round of fake laughter—and Chelsea and Eddie shared a worried glance. From the looks of things, it was only a matter of time before these air-kissin' cousins started cracking each other's heads.

* * *

Later that night, as everyone got ready for bed, Raven's little brother found himself following his father to the living room. And Cory was *not* happy about it. "When I said Andrea could sleep in my room, you did not *tell* me I had to sleep on the *couch*," Cory complained.

"Oh, come on, Cory," said Mr. Baxter, setting a pile of blankets on the sofa bed. "Think of it as an adventure. It'll be fun down here, all by yourself." A prankish grin crossed Mr. Baxter's face. "But whatever you do," he added in a playfully spooky tone, "*d-o-o-n't* open the coat closet. 'Cause you never know what might be hiding in there."

"What is hiding in there?" asked Cory, his eyes widening in fear.

Mr. Baxter stared at his son in disbelief. He'd only been kidding. Cory couldn't *really* be scared, could he?

But Cory was already racing back up the

stairs. "No way! No way!" he cried in terror.

"Cory!" called Mr. Baxter. "It was a joke!"

An hour later, Cory lay sprawled in his parents' bed, snoring loudly. Wide awake, his mother and father lay on their backs, staring at the ceiling.

"'Don't open the coat closet'?" Mrs. Baxter whispered in disgust.

"It was a joke!" Mr. Baxter insisted helplessly.

Just then, Cory rolled over and snored right into his father's ear. Mr. Baxter groaned. Mrs. Baxter sighed. It may have been a joke, but nobody in this bed was laughing.

Chapter Three

The next morning, Raven energetically paced the kitchen floor. Operation Stick Eddie With Her Stuck-up Cousin was about to get underway.

"Okay, now," she told Eddie, who was sitting at the kitchen table, "when Andrea comes downstairs, I'm going to say that I can't do anything after school because I'm busy. That's where you come in."

"Then I kiss her?" he asked, his head eagerly bobbing up and down.

"No, Eddie," said Raven. "*Then* you ask her to do something after school."

"Right, right. *Then* I kiss her?" he asked again.

Raven rolled her eyes. "No," she told him a second time. "Then you take her out. Get to know her. Make her laugh—"

Eddie stared blankly at Raven. *Dang*, thought Raven. Head bobbing, drooling, puppy-dog eyes—will someone get this boy a leash? Shaking her head, Raven finally threw Eddie his bone.

"*Then* you kiss her," she told him.

Eddie grinned. Moments later, Andrea sashayed into the room.

"*Bonjour, mes amis,*" she called haughtily.

Oh, come off it, Raven wanted to tell her. Why can't you just say "What's up?" like a *normal* person?

As soon as he saw Andrea, Eddie practically leaped over to the "kissing spot" by the kitchen table. "Oh, hi," he said casually. "I just dropped by to see if Raven wanted to walk to school."

"Oh, Eddie, I would love to," Raven gushed. "But if you're thinking about doing anything *after* school, I can't. 'Cause, you know, I'm busy."

"Oh, *please*," said Andrea, "you don't have to tell me about busy. I'm head of the Honor Society, and I still have to find time to edit the yearbook."

"Very interesting," muttered Raven, seething with jealousy. "Well, I barely have time to *read* the yearbook, because I'm head of the volleyball team and head of, you know, the . . . cheerleaders' . . . society."

Eddie gave Raven a confused look. "The cheerleaders' society?" he whispered.

"Yes. It's new," Raven explained, loud enough for Andrea to hear. "We . . . we . . . you know, we cheer for the . . . elderly. It raises their spirits. We go, like . . ." Raven raised her arms, gave an awkward kick, and shouted,

"Go-o-o, Old People!" Then she lost her balance and stumbled to the floor.

Andrea's eyebrows rose skeptically as Raven stood up and brushed herself off.

"You know, Ravey," said Andrea, "since you're so busy later, maybe I'll just go to school with you right now."

Raven tried to smile—but when Andrea turned her back, Raven's grin changed into a grimace. Operation Stick Eddie had suddenly backfired. And now Raven was stuck.

By that afternoon, Raven was ready to scream. All day, her cousin had been dazzling Raven's classmates with glamorous tales of living in Europe. Instead of seeing Andrea as the phoniest of phonies, the fools hung on to her every word!

And now, just down the hall, it was happening again. A group of students had surrounded Raven's chic cousin. Green with envy, Raven and Chelsea watched the whole scene.

"So there I was," Andrea told the students, gesturing dramatically, "just walking along the Champs d'Elysee when this photographer walks up to me and says, 'Aren't you Tyra Banks?'" Andrea and all the kids around her laughed.

"Look at her," said Raven, chomping the life out of a stick of gum. "She's been like that all day. Everybody thinks she so cool 'cause she eats in Europe, shops in Europe, goes to school in Europe—"

"Okay, we get it, Rae," Chelsea interrupted. "Europe thing—not good."

"This has been the *worst* day I've ever had," complained Raven, as she and Chelsea dragged themselves down the hall.

"I'm having the *best* day ever!" cried Andrea, rushing up to them.

"Girl, me too," lied Raven, giving her cousin a big phony smile. Just then, a group of Bayside Junior High cheerleaders bounded down the school stairs and clustered around a nearby locker.

"Hey, Ravey," said Andrea with a nasty look in her eye, "why don't you introduce me to your cheerleading squad since *you're* the captain?"

"Right," said Raven uneasily. She could tell by her cousin's tone that she didn't believe it. Well, believe this, thought Raven. "Let's go meet the girls. Come on."

Raven marched right over to the group of cheerleaders. "Hey, squad, what's going on?" she asked brightly. "I made up a new cheer. Okay, diamond position, girls . . ." Throwing her arms into the air, Raven shouted, "Two! Four! Six! Eight! That is the way we like to . . . count! Uh . . . Angie, work on that. Amber, you need some help, okay?"

The cheerleaders stared at Raven in complete confusion. But before they could ask, *Who are you and what do you think you're doing?* Raven quickly walked away.

"So, where's Eddie?" Raven asked as she led Andrea and Chelsea down the hall—*away* from the cheerleaders. "Because after school, I've got a million other things to do."

A group of cute guys passed by and Andrea waved at them. "Oh, *bonjour*, guys," she called. "How's it going?"

With huge smiles, the guys waved back and replied, *"Bonjour!"*

Raven's fists clenched. My stupid cousin visits my stupid school for one day, she fumed, and half the stupid boys are suddenly speaking French!

"American boys are so cute," Andrea said with a little sigh. "If only I didn't have Jean-Paul waiting for me back in Paris. Oh, he misses me so much. You know how *boyfriends* are, Ravey . . . Oh, I'm sorry. You don't."

"Actually, I *do* know how boyfriends are," Raven lied.

"Yeah, she does," Chelsea agreed, backing up her best friend.

"Yeah, 'cause I have one," declared Raven.

"Yeah, she does," Chelsea repeated.

"And he makes your Jean-Paul look like French toast," Raven added.

"French toast!" echoed Chelsea.

"'Cause he is charming and cute, and he is there for me. And he is—" Just then, Raven noticed a familiar boy walking toward them— the perfect boy to play the part of her perfect boyfriend. "Eddie," she declared.

"Eddie?" Chelsea repeated in surprise.

"Bon Jovi, y'all," said Eddie, walking up to them.

Raven cringed. That boy is just never going

to get the foreign language thing, she thought. But, at the moment, it didn't matter. To Raven, all that mattered was making Andrea believe she had the better boyfriend.

Quickly, Raven slipped her arm around Eddie's shoulders and gushed, "Oh, boyfriend, you say the cutest things. Come on, Boo."

"Who's Boo?" Eddie asked as they strolled away.

Raven didn't want to scare her friend, but she had to explain. "Boo is *you*."

Chapter Four

"**O**kay, okay," Raven told Eddie that night on the phone, "I know I shouldn't have said we were going out, but she made me so mad. Can't you just be my boyfriend for one week? What's the big deal?"

"Because in a week, Andrea will be gone," said Eddie. "You had a vision. Now I have that same vision. I *want* that kiss. You *promised* me that kiss."

"I'm sorry," said Raven, "but if I back out now, she will never let me live it down."

"But I'm a man," said Eddie. "I have feelings. I need to be held, Rae."

Raven hated it when Eddie whined— especially when he was refusing to help her get what she wanted. "Okay, Eddie," she snapped, "don't make me come over there and—" Raven froze when she noticed Andrea walking through the door of her attic bedroom. "Give you the biggest hug my Eddie Bear has ever had," Raven quickly finished, loud enough for Andrea to hear.

"What?" cried Eddie on other end of the phone. But a second later, he understood. "She's there, isn't she?"

"Oh, I miss you, too, Pookie," Raven cooed into the phone.

"Okay now, Rae, that's it," complained Eddie. "I'm drawing the line at 'Pookie.'"

"Hey," said Andrea, sitting down next to Raven, "you think Eddie would want to come over for dinner tomorrow night?"

"I'd love to! I'd love to! I'd love to! I'd love to! I'd love to!" Eddie shouted. Raven held the receiver against her chest, smothering

Eddie's voice, and stared innocently at Andrea.

"He says he's kind of busy," Raven replied.

"Let *me* talk to him," insisted Andrea. She reached for the phone, but Raven wouldn't let go. Andrea pulled. Raven pulled right back. Andrea *yanked* with all her strength—and the phone broke free of Raven's grip.

"Eddie, it's Andrea," she said. "Listen, I insist you join us for dinner tomorrow—"

"I'd love to!" cried Eddie, then he immediately hung up before Raven could *un*-invite him.

Andrea held the phone out to Raven, then stood up. "Well," she said, "seems he just can't say no to me. And, as a special treat, I'll cook dinner."

Raven got up, too. "That won't be necessary," she said, facing off with the Queen of Chic, "because I'm an *excellent* cook. And no one cooks for my man but *me*. Good night."

With fake air-kisses flying, Raven and Andrea parted for the night.

That night, when Andrea went back to Cory's bedroom, Cory went back to his parents' bed. For the second night in a row, Mr. and Mrs. Baxter found themselves wide-awake, staring at the ceiling and listening to their son snore like a water buffalo.

Suddenly, the room was quiet. For a few minutes, the sleeping Cory actually stopped snoring—only to stretch out his arms and whack both of his parents in the head.

That was the last straw. "Sofa bed?" Mr. Baxter quietly suggested to his wife.

She gave him a sour look. "As long as you don't 'open the coat closet,'" she snapped.

"It was a *joke*," Mr. Baxter insisted for the hundredth time.

Shaking her head, Mrs. Baxter threw off the

covers. "Come on," she said. Together, they trudged down to the living room, opened up the sofa bed, and made the mattress up with sheets and blankets. Finally, they settled comfortably under the covers.

They had just closed their eyes when they heard a voice—

"I woke up, and you weren't there!"

"Please let this be a dream," Mr. Baxter whispered, his eyes still closed.

No such luck. Lifting his eyelids, he saw Cory dive onto the sofa bed.

"Snuggle up to your *father*," Mrs. Baxter said with a sigh.

Cory happily did. A few minutes later, he was snoring loudly once again.

But that wasn't the worst of it. All night long, Cory shifted this way and that. First, his arms were in their faces. Next, his feet were on their pillows. Then, he stole all the covers, and finally, he sprawled his whole body out. His parents were forced to cling, shivering and coverless, to the edges of the bed.

By the end of the seemingly endless night, Cory's parents had been twisted into two miserable pretzels—while Cory slept like a log.

Chapter Five

By the next evening, Raven had cooked up a plan to impress Andrea . . . and it *didn't* involve cooking. She sent Chelsea to pick up a fancy meal from a nearby restaurant. Then she tied on a chef's apron and placed half a dozen pots and pans on the stove, just to make it look like she was a culinary genius.

I'm totally set to fake out my totally fake cousin, thought Raven. If only my fake boyfriend would adjust his attitude and get with the program.

"First, you tell me that Andrea is going to kiss me," Eddie complained. "Then, you make me your boyfriend, so I can't kiss her. Man, this is one big psychic rip-off!"

"You think it's easy being your girl?" Raven retorted, stirring a pot full of boiling water. "You don't take me anywhere. You don't buy me anything. It's not like I got ice," she said, pointing to her diamond-free neck. "I slave over a hot stove, and all you do is nag, nag, nag."

Eddie took a step back. Raven was acting like they were *actually* dating. "Okay, Rae," he said, "this is really starting to get weird." Then he shrugged and looked at the pots. "So, what's for dinner, *sweetheart*?"

"Stuffed Crab Imperial," Raven announced proudly. "Chelsea's down at the Sea Lion restaurant picking it up."

Eddie's jaw dropped. "Then what's all this boiling water?" he asked.

"Well, I've got to create the *illusion* that I'm cooking," Raven explained.

She peered into one of the pots. "You know,

that water needs a dash more salt," she announced, lobbing a pinch of it into the water. "Bam!"

Eddie took *another* step back. This girl was getting into her fake cooking just a little *too* much, he decided.

Just then, the back doorknob rattled and the door flew open. It was Chelsea, holding a huge box of food.

Raven ran to greet her. "So, how'd everything go at the restaurant?" she asked Chelsea excitedly.

"Well, actually—" Chelsea began, but Raven suddenly slammed the door in her face. Andrea was coming down the back staircase, and Raven could *not* let her see those restaurant containers.

"Ravey, how's everything going down here?" asked Andrea. She was dressed exquisitely, of course—white pants, a white top covered by a lacy blouse, and a matching white beret.

Eddie stared. But Andrea didn't notice. She was more interested in checking on Raven's dinner. She pulled on the oven door and was about to peek inside. But, with a well-aimed kick, Raven slammed the door shut.

"Ah-ah-ah," said Raven. "No peeking." She guided Andrea and Eddie toward the kitchen door. "I think we all need to go into the dining room and get settled," she suggested.

As Andrea moved toward the dinner table, Raven caught Eddie's arm. "All right, *boyfriend*," she rasped into his ear, "tell me you love me."

"No," said Eddie.

"Well, then say I look pretty," she pleaded.

"No," he repeated.

"Say *something* nice," she begged.

"Your cousin looks hot tonight," Eddie

whispered. Then he broke away from Raven and rushed over to the table. "Let me get that for you," he told Andrea, pulling out her chair.

"You are so thoughtful," cooed Andrea, sitting down. "Thank you, Edward."

"Oh, you're very welcome," Eddie said with a grin.

"Hey, is dinner ready?" called Cory, running up to the table and taking his seat.

"Just about," said Raven. She glanced at her parents, who slowly followed Cory into the room. Raven's parents looked like mirror images of each other. Mr. Baxter's head was twisted painfully to the right, and Mrs. Baxter's head was twisted uncomfortably to the left.

"You guys feeling any better?" Raven asked them, wincing.

"Not much," said Mrs. Baxter. "That sofa bed really messed up our necks."

"I don't know why," said Cory with a care-free shrug. "'Cause I slept like a baby."

With a very great effort, Mr. and Mrs. Baxter turned their heads far enough to give their snoring little angel an exasperated look.

"We know!" they cried in unison.

Chapter Six

When Raven returned to the kitchen, she found Chelsea spooning side dishes out of the aluminum take-out containers and onto the dinner plates.

Raven sighed with relief. "Thank you so much, Chelsea," she told her friend. "Oh my goodness, this looks so good. Rice Almondine. Fresh vegetables . . ." Raven glanced around, but she didn't see the main dish. "Okay, where's the Crab Imperial?"

Chelsea gave her best friend a guilty look. "In the box," she said nervously.

Raven didn't like the sound of that. She walked over to the kitchen table, where a big cardboard box was sitting. Do not *tell* me I am looking at a box of *live* crabs, Raven thought, peering inside.

"Chels," said Raven, trying not to freak.

"I know," said Chelsea. "That awful restaurant. They wanted to *kill* them. And I saved them. Look, look, look," she cried, running over to the box. "I saved Fred and Ethel . . . and Little Ricky."

Raven lifted the squirming "Little Ricky" from the box and examined him. "You know what, Chelsea?" said Raven. "It's okay, 'cause I understand that you love the animals. And I'm all for it, girl. I respect that." Still holding the crab, Raven slowly began to move across the kitchen.

"Rae, what'cha doin'?" Chelsea asked suspiciously.

"I'm just showing it around the kitchen," said Raven brightly. "You know, here's the kitchen. Here's the refrigerator . . . and here's the hot pot of boiling water!"

But before Raven could drop Little Ricky in, Chelsea grabbed Raven's arm. "Rae, you can't!" she yelled.

"I have to!" said Raven. "I've got my snotty cousin in there to impress." She looked at Little Ricky. "Sorry, crabby."

"No, no, no, no!" cried Chelsea.

The two girls continued to fight over the crab, until they lost their balance. They fell to the floor with a loud *crash*!

"Everything okay in there?" Mrs. Baxter called from the dining room.

In the kitchen, Raven and Chelsea scrambled to their feet. The crab's claws were now tangled in their hair.

"Fine!" Raven hollered to her mother. "I cannot believe this crab is attached to our heads," she snapped at Chelsea.

"Rae, Rae, Rae," Chelsea said soothingly, "remember, he's more scared of us than we are of him."

"We're getting hungry out here!" shouted Mr. Baxter.

"We're coming!" Raven shouted back. Then she whispered desperately to Chelsea, "What are we going to do?"

"There are scissors over there," suggested Chelsea. Together they crossed over to the counter and grabbed the scissors.

"Okay, we'll cut your hair, Rae," said Chelsea, holding up the blades.

"What?" cried Raven. "I'm sorry, why can't we cut *yours*?"

"All right. Scissors—bad idea," pronounced Chelsea.

A few moments later, Raven and Chelsea came up with another solution. With the crab hidden behind their heads, they walked into the dining room plastered to each other as if they were joined at the hip.

"Look who came to help me serve the salad!" announced Raven with forced cheerfulness.

"Yes," Chelsea said stiffly. "No one serves salad like I do."

"Ravey, do you need any help in the kitchen?" Andrea asked from her seat at the dining room table.

"Oh, no," insisted Raven. "Everything's under control."

Raven and Chelsea walked around the dinner table, serving the salad together. Raven held the bowl with her right hand—and, using a pair of tongs, Chelsea served everyone with her left. All the while, the girls' *other* hands were busy hiding the crab behind their heads!

"All right, here's some for Mr. Baxter," said

Chelsea, dipping the tongs into the bowl and dropping a pile of greens onto his plate. "And some for Mrs. Baxter. And here's some for—" Suddenly, the crab's claw pulled at Chelsea's hair. In a high-pitched squeal, she shouted, "Cory!"

Cory grinned and turned to Andrea. "She always gets a little emotional when she says my name," he explained.

Chelsea ignored him and kept serving. "Eddie, there you go," she said. Finally, she served Andrea.

"And your main dish will be right up," announced Raven.

"What are we having, anyway?" asked Andrea.

"Girl, we are having crab. Really, really *fresh* crab," Raven said. "Okay, your salad servers will be leaving now."

"Buh-bye, buh-bye, buh-bye, see ya,"

Raven and Chelsea chirped as they backed out the door together.

At the dinner table, Eddie began to shovel salad into his mouth. Suddenly, Andrea turned to him and batted her long eyelashes. "Raven is *so* lucky to have a guy like you," she cooed.

Eddie froze. That was the last thing he'd expected to hear. His mouth still crammed with salad, he garbled, "She is?"

Back in the kitchen, Chelsea and Raven kept working on their crab detangling.

"Almost . . ." said Chelsea. "Okay, I think I've got it, Rae! One, two . . . three! I'm free!" Chelsea stumbled backward.

"I'm so happy for you," muttered Raven, holding up the crab that was still attached to her hair. "Can you help me?"

But before Chelsea could do a thing, Eddie rushed into the room. "Rae," he said, "I think your cousin's coming on to me . . . and you've got a crab in your hair."

"I know," said Raven, embarrassed. She held it up like a seashell comb and batted her eyelashes. "How do you like it?"

"We don't want Andrea to see her like this," said Chelsea. "Go watch the door."

"You know what?" Raven complained to Eddie as Chelsea struggled to remove the crab. "That is *just* like Andrea. As soon as she finds out that you're my boyfriend, she's all over you!"

"Yo, Andrea's coming," warned Eddie, peeking through the curtain covering the kitchen door.

"Oh, I can't let her see me like this!" Raven cried in a panic. "Here, take it."

Handing the crab to Chelsea, Raven dropped behind the counter in the center of the kitchen. The end of her long braid was still tangled in the crab's claws. As Andrea entered, Chelsea quickly dropped the crab onto a dinner plate sitting on the counter.

"Are you sure there's nothing I can do?" asked Andrea, taking in the scene.

"No," said Chelsea.

"I'll help cook the crab," Andrea suggested, grabbing the live crab off the dinner plate in front of Chelsea.

Beneath the counter, Raven felt the yank on her braid. Her head slammed into the underside of the counter. *Bang!*

"No, you're the guest," protested Chelsea, pulling the crab right back. Down dropped Raven's head.

"No, I'll help," insisted Andrea, yanking once more. And, once more, *bang!* went Raven's head.

"No, you're the guest," Chelsea told Andrea, pulling the crab back.

Finally, Andrea backed off. "Where's Raven?" she asked.

"Raven? Where is she?" Chelsea stalled. "Uh, she's upstairs. She and Eddie just had a big fight and broke up."

Under the counter, Raven angrily poked Chelsea.

Just then, Raven's parents entered the kitchen. "What's taking so long?" Mrs. Baxter asked.

"Are those *restaurant* containers?" Mr. Baxter asked, spying the aluminum tins on the counter.

Andrea turned to her aunt and uncle. "It sounds like Eddie and Raven broke up," she said.

"What?" Mr. and Mrs. Baxter cried, stunned. Their heads whipped toward her so fast, they cracked the cricks right out of their sore necks.

"Raven and Eddie aren't going out," said

Mr. Baxter, rubbing his neck. "'Cause if they were, Eddie would have told us." Frowning, the big man walked over to Eddie and put a beefy arm around his neck. "Isn't that right, son?"

"Uh, Rae," Eddie squeaked uneasily, "little help here!"

Raven slowly stood up from beneath the counter. She finally pulled her braid free of the stupid crab. With a *plop*, she dropped the crustacean onto the plate.

"Hey, everybody . . ." she said weakly, trying not to die of total humiliation. "Enjoy the salads?"

"What is going on?" demanded her father.

"Okay, Eddie and I aren't dating," she told her family. "It was all a joke. Just like this dinner. All to impress her." She pointed to Andrea. "So, here, Eddie, you want her? You can have her."

Raven grabbed the two of them and pulled them to the "kissing spot" from her vision. Then she turned and ran up the stairs to her room.

Eddie glanced at Andrea. It was the moment he'd been waiting for. But right then, something more important was on his mind. "I've got to see if Rae is okay," he told Andrea.

But before he could go, Andrea yanked him back.

"No," she said, turning toward the stairs. "This is between my cousin and me."

Chapter Seven

In her bedroom, Raven sat down at the one place where she could always make her problems fade away—her sewing machine.

But she soon found out this problem wasn't going away. Instead, it walked right through her bedroom door.

"I think we need to talk," said Andrea.

"Why's that?" asked Raven. "Are you here to brag about something else and make me feel worse about my life? Look, I'll save you the trouble, okay?" Taking a deep breath, Raven stood up and faced her cousin. "I lied," she confessed. "I'm not head of the volleyball squad. I'm not the head cheerleader. And I can't cook. So congratulations, you win. Your life is better than mine."

Pushing past Andrea, Raven ran out her bedroom door and down the back staircase. She wanted to apologize to Eddie and her family for spoiling dinner. But when she got to the kitchen, everyone had already cleared out.

"Rae, hold on," said Andrea, rushing to catch up to her cousin. Raven turned around. "You actually think *my* life is better than *yours*?" Andrea asked.

"You sure make it seem that way," said Raven.

"Well, it's not," Andrea told her. "I live in a different country every year. I change homes, I have to make new friends. . . . Believe me, Rae, you don't know how lucky you are."

But Raven *didn't* believe her. "I don't shop in Rome, okay?" she told her cousin. "I don't live in Paris."

"Yeah, well, I'd trade all that for this," admitted Andrea, gesturing to the walls of the Baxters' home. She walked over to the kitchen doorframe, where little pencil marks recorded Raven and Cory's heights since they'd been old enough to stand.

"You were standing right here when you were two and four and seven and nine," said Andrea, pointing to the little slashes on the wood. "I don't have that. I don't have a real home like you do. Oh, and you'll really love this one. I don't have a boyfriend either. I made him up to impress you, because I thought you had the better life." She shrugged. "So I don't win, *you* do."

Raven shook her head. She could *not* believe what she was hearing. *How stupid*, she thought. "You mean, we wasted fourteen years trying to impress each other when we could've been friends?" she said.

Andrea nodded, and Raven sighed. Then she asked, "Want to start over?"

"Sure," said Andrea with a big smile.

Raven smiled back, then she pursed her lips in thought. "You know that red bag you had on the other day?" she asked. "Can I borrow it?"

"Only if you tell me where you got those shoes," said Andrea.

"Girl, they were on sale!" squealed Raven.

The two girls hugged. Then, for the first time in their lives, when they kissed each other's cheeks, no air was involved.

A short time later, the two cousins were sitting at the kitchen counter, laughing and eating ice cream out of the same container.

"You remember that pony I had?" asked Andrea.

"Yeah," said Raven.

"Made it up!" Andrea admitted.

"Remember my soccer trophy?" asked Raven.

Andrea nodded.

"Garage sale," said Raven.

The two girls burst out laughing as Eddie pushed open the kitchen door.

"I'm glad to see you guys worked everything out," he said.

"So are we," they agreed in unison.

"Well, I'm leaving," he told them. "Thanks for dinner. I've got to go home and *eat*."

Eddie started for the back door, but as he passed the kitchen table, Raven called out, "Eddie, wait."

Eddie stopped and waited while Raven whispered something into Andrea's ear. After everything Raven had put Eddie through, she figured she couldn't let her best friend leave her house without a little dessert.

Andrea smiled at Raven's whispered suggestion, then she got up and walked over to Eddie. Leaning in, she took his chin in her hand and puckered up. The next thing Eddie knew, his "little French pastry" was laying a supersweet kiss on him!

Dazed, Eddie just stood there, unable to move. He barely even noticed when the two girls giggled, waved, and then left the room.

At last Eddie came to and looked around. He was standing in the "kissing spot," just like in Raven's vision. A big grin spread across Eddie's face as he threw his fist in the air and hollered in triumph, "I love this spot!"

that's SO raven

Part Two

Chapter One

Raven marched angrily into the kitchen. "Cory," she snapped at her little brother, "have you been using my CD player again?"

Cory looked up from his cereal bowl, eyes wide. "No," he said innocently.

Raven flipped open the CD player. "Then why is there baloney in it?" she asked, holding up a round slice of lunch meat with a perfect hole cut out of the middle.

"Are you mad?" asked Cory.

Raven's eyes narrowed. "You got that right," she snapped.

Cory's face broke out in a devilish grin. "Then it's done its job," he said.

One look at that grin, and Raven lost it.

"Look, toad—" she snarled, ready to launch an all-out attack. But her father, who'd been searching through the fridge, stopped her.

"Hey, hey, that's enough out of you two!" he shouted, pointing a warning finger. "Don't make me turn this . . . er . . ." He glanced around. *Whoops!* They weren't in the car. "*Kitchen* around. 'Cause I will," he finished lamely.

On the other side of the counter, Raven's mother just shook her head. She was busy icing Cory's birthday cake. "Okay, Cory," Mrs. Baxter said, changing the subject, "have you thought about what friends you want to bring to the movies for your birthday tomorrow?"

Cory shrugged. "Just Stevie and Mark," he said, but he didn't sound all that excited about it.

"That's all?" asked his father, walking over

to the counter. "You sure you don't want to do something a little more *special*?"

"Why bother?" said Cory with a shake of his head. "Every year Billy Correll has his party the day before mine. And everybody always likes it better."

Still fuming over the baloney prank, Raven snapped, "Hey, Cory, did you ever consider that maybe it's not the *party* they like better?"

A fleeting look of hurt crossed Cory's face. He was used to trading insults with his sister. But Raven had hit below the belt with that one. It took him a second to reply.

"Well," he finally said, pointing to the flower in Raven's hair, "how would you like me to make that flower a *permanent* part of your head?"

"Can you *reach* it?" she teased, leaning over her shorter brother then straightening up so the flower was out of reach.

Cory jumped, ready to tear the thing right out of his sister's hair, but Mr. Baxter quickly stepped between them. "Okay, okay, okay, that's enough, you two!" he declared.

With a grunt of fury, Cory stormed out of the kitchen. Mr. Baxter turned to face Raven. She could see the man was *not* happy.

"Why do you always have to get in his face like that?" her father asked. "You're his big sister. You should know better."

Raven blew it off with a wave of her hand. "Dad, this is part of the morning routine," she said. "Take a bath, brush my teeth, fight with Cory, eat a muffin." To make her point, she opened her mouth and shoved a blueberry muffin into it.

Across the room, Raven's mother spoke up. "Honey, you remember Lucy Sherman? You two were the best of friends until third grade.

And then for some reason, you started *picking* at each other."

Raven swallowed the bite of muffin and rolled her eyes. "Mom," she said, "what does *she* have to do with anything? We don't even talk anymore."

"You *don't?*" said her mother. "Oh, *gee*, did I just make a point?"

"You think that's actually going to happen with me and Cory?" Raven asked. "Mama, *please*. He's probably upstairs right now putting hot dogs in my blow dryer."

Suddenly, Raven froze. Her eyes opened wide, her skin began to tingle, and the world around her seemed to stop in time . . .

Through her eye
The vision runs
Flash of future
Here it comes—

I see my little brother, Cory. He's standing in our living room, near our front door wearing his black-and-yellow shirt and . . . an Australian bush hat?

Uh-oh, looks like I'm in this vision, too. I'm standing a few feet away. For some reason, Cory looks all hurt and disappointed, like he's about to cry.

But he doesn't cry. Instead, he takes off the bush hat and throws it to the floor—wow, he is SO upset. Now he's starting to yell in a really angry voice—

"You're the worst sister. I hate you!"

Raven shook her head clear of the psychic vision. Tuning back in, she heard her father's deep voice warn, ". . . All we're saying is that one day you're going to push him a little too far."

Raven gulped.

Chapter Two

"I've never had a vision like this before, you guys," Raven told Chelsea and Eddie after school that day, as they lounged in Raven's attic bedroom. "Cory said that I was the worst sister, and that he hated me."

Eddie shook his head. "Rae, my brother says he hates me all the time," he told her. "It doesn't *mean* anything."

Raven put her hands on her hips. "Eddie, your brother is *two*, okay?" she pointed out. "All he *can* say is, 'I hate you' and 'I have poopie in my pants.'"

From the bed, Chelsea piped up, "Rae, maybe you're making too big a deal out of this."

"You guys did not see this look on his face,

okay?" Raven told her friends. "I have never seen him so angry at me before. What if he never talks to me again?"

"Oh right," said Chelsea, "and that would be a *bad* thing?" She and Eddie started to laugh.

"Funny, huh," said Chelsea, when Raven didn't join in.

Raven gave them both a searing glare. "This is not a joke, you guys," she said. "This is my little brother, and I just can't have him hate me."

Eddie and Chelsea stopped laughing. They could see this was important to their best friend. The only question was, if Cory was destined to hate Raven, what could she possibly do about it?

That evening, Raven found Cory watching TV in the living room. "Look who's home,"

Raven said in a voice as sweet as honey. "Looks like *someone* needs a little pillow fluffing."

Cory eyed his sister suspiciously as she fluffed a couch pillow then tenderly set it behind his head.

"There you go!" Raven exclaimed. "Can't hate a pillow-fluffer, can you?"

Cory looked at Raven like she'd lost her mind. His eyes followed her as she moved around the couch and sat down next to him. He was sure she was up to some sort of prank—he just hadn't figured out exactly *what* yet.

"So, how was your day?" Raven asked him sincerely.

"We all went to the aquarium for Billy's birthday and had a great time," Cory told her. "I *hated* it."

"Aww," said Raven. "Well, maybe a little candy will make it all better." She whipped out a giant-sized chocolate bar and held it out to him.

Cory eagerly took the bar, then stopped. He cast a wary glance at Raven and put the bar up to his nose to sniff for sabotage. Hot pepper flakes could not be ruled out, he decided. She could have dipped the bar in dishwashing liquid or replaced the almonds with laxatives.

Cory pushed the bar back at his big sister. "*You* take the first bite," he told her.

Just then, Mr. and Mrs. Baxter came down the stairs, dressed for an evening out. "We won't be gone too long," Raven's father announced. "We're going to walk down to that new seafood restaurant for dinner."

Raven's mother draped a lace shawl around her shoulders. "You go to bed early, honey," she told Cory. "You've got a big birthday tomorrow."

Cory nodded, and his parents headed for

the front door. "Oh, and take a bath," Mrs. Baxter called over her shoulder.

Cory rolled his eyes.

"With soap," his mother added, "and water. And *don't* put that same underwear back on."

Cory glanced at Raven, embarrassed, and sank down into the couch cushions.

"Don't feel bad, son," Mr. Baxter called as he followed Mrs. Baxter out the door. "Your mama tells me the same thing." Then they were gone.

Sighing, Cory went back to watching TV— and ignoring his big sister.

But Raven hadn't given up on him yet. Jumping to her feet, she cried, "Wow, Cory, your tenth birthday. And you know what you need? You need a 'my party's better than Billy's party' party. And *I'm* going to give it to you."

"Really?" said Cory, still skeptical.

"Mmm-hmm," she assured him.

Cory eyed her closely. "What's in it for you?" he asked.

"Just to know that I'm the one who put a beautiful smile on your face," said Raven.

"Well, if that's all you want," said Cory, "you can just move out!"

Gladly, if it would get me away from your ugly face, Raven almost snapped back. But she stopped herself. That vision of her little brother saying he hated her was going to come true unless she did something about it. And that something did *not* include acting like the wicked witch of the living room.

"I *could* move out," Raven carefully replied, "but then you would miss that great party I'm going to throw for you."

Cory thought about his sister's offer for a moment. "What *kind* of party?" he asked, feeling a little hopeful that she wasn't totally putting him on.

"I don't know yet. But whatever it is, I promise you, you won't hate me—it," she corrected quickly. "You won't hate *it*." Or me, Raven added silently. Or me.

For the rest of that night, Raven helped Cory phone all of his friends and invite them over the next day for the greatest party ever. When Mr. and Mrs. Baxter arrived home, Raven sat down with them, and together they came up with the party's theme. Then her father made a quick phone call to a good friend who worked at the San Francisco Zoo. And by the time they went to bed, everything was set.

Dang! Raven thought, lying in bed that night. This is really going to happen. Tomorrow I officially become the greatest sister *ever*!

Chapter Three

Ding-dong!

Raven raced to open the door for the ninth time. A group of boys stood on the Baxters' front porch, holding presents for Cory.

"Hey, y'all!" Raven exclaimed with a great big smile. "Welcome to Cory's tenth-birthday party. It's going to be the bomb. Come on in!"

A large group of kids had already arrived at the Baxters' house and were now munching on snacks in the living room. Raven waved in the new kids. As the line of boys tramped across the threshold, she used her expert shopper's eye to scan every wrapped box they carried. Suddenly, she tapped one boy on his shoulder.

"I'll take that present," she told him, holding out her hand. The kid handed it over. "Thank you!" Raven chirped. Then she held the gift to her ear and shook it. "Sounds cheap, sweetie," she whispered to her brother. "I'll get you something better."

Raven was doing everything possible to make sure Cory's birthday turned out perfect in every way. The "gift check" was just the beginning.

She grinned at two new boys walking through the front door. "Hey, all right," she called to them.

Cory recognized the two boys. The tall one was Billy Correll, the kid who *always* had a better birthday party than Cory's. And the red-headed one was Billy's best friend, Jaime.

"There's no way your party's going to be better than mine," Billy announced tauntingly.

Raven's eyes narrowed. *Where does this kid get his* attitude, *she wondered in disgust.*

"Well, *actually*," she declared loudly, "my brother's birthday party is going to be *tight*, thank you very much. . . . Tell him where we're going," she whispered to Cory.

"We're going to the San Francisco Zoo," said Cory.

"The zoo?" said Jaime, unimpressed. "*That's your great idea?*"

Raven scowled at the redhead. "Zip it, okay?" she told him. "'Cause he's not finished." She turned back to Cory. "*Finish*," she told him.

"My dad got us VIP passes to the Reptile House," Cory announced to the room full of kids. "We get to party with the pythons!"

The kids all leaped up, waved their hands in the air, and gave a deafening cheer. "Go, Cory! Go, Cory! Go, Cory!" they began to chant.

Cory's grin was so wide, Raven nearly cried with joy. She had never seen her little brother so happy!

"Rae," said Cory, "you're the best."

And she'd certainly never heard him say those words before, either!

"I know I am," Raven told him, "'Cause I'm your sister. And you love me. Now, keep that thought. I'm going to go get Mom and Dad so we can go to the zoo!"

With "Go, Cory!" ringing in her ears, Raven raced up the stairs. But when she opened her parents' bedroom door, she couldn't believe her eyes. Her mother and father weren't even *close* to being ready.

"What are you guys still doing in bed?" she cried. "Get dressed, we've got to go to the zoo!"

As Raven turned to leave, she heard a

terrible groan. *Uh-oh*, she thought, I don't like the sound of that. Slowly, she turned back around and took another look at her folks. Their faces were contorted in pain.

"Your mom and I got food poisoning from the seafood restaurant last night," her father explained, holding his head and rubbing his stomach.

Raven's mom dragged herself into a sitting position on the mattress. "You know that left-over linguine with clams we brought home?" she said. "Throw it out."

Suddenly, Raven's mom looked more than a little queasy. "Did I say 'throw'?" she asked. A moment later, she was leaping from the bed, arms flailing. She lunged for the bathroom and slammed the door shut behind her.

Raven's father crawled out of bed. "We're going to have to cancel Cory's party," he told Raven. Crossing to the bathroom, Mr. Baxter

"I just need to know which hat says,
'Thanks for coming, but you need
to go back to Paris,' " said Raven.

"This is my kissing face," said Eddie.

"Look at her," Raven said. "Everybody thinks she's so cool."

"Who's Boo?" Eddie asked.

"Ah-ah-ah," Raven said, slamming the oven door shut. "No peeking."

"I cannot believe this crab is attached to our heads," Raven snapped.

**"Raven is so lucky to have a guy like you,"
Andrea cooed.**

**The next thing Eddie knew, his "little French
pastry" was laying a supersweet kiss on him!**

"Why is there baloney in it?" Raven asked.

"You take the first bite," Cory told Raven.

"Voila!" cried Raven. "Iguana!"

"My head's starting to feel a little clammy.
Do I look okay?" Mr. Baxter asked.

"Raven Baxter is modeling this year's newest fall fashion," Chelsea declared.

"I guess that's why it hasn't been eating the mice," said Raven.

"So, we're okay?" Raven asked.

"Raven!"

knocked on the door. "Honey?" he called to his wife.

This can't be happening, thought Raven. This is worse than my vision—this is a waking *nightmare*!

"Dad, we *cannot* cancel Cory's party, okay?" she told him. "He is going to *hate* me."

"No, he won't—" her father began, then he stopped. Suddenly, he looked queasy, too. And when he glanced at the locked bathroom door, he also began to look panicked.

Walking over to Raven, he put his hands on her shoulders. "Now, you're a psychic, right, baby?" he asked desperately. "Tell me how long your mama's going to be in there!"

Breaking free, Raven ran out the door. Her parents were out of the picture—so it was up to her to break the worst news ever to her baby brother.

And, no matter what her father said, she just knew he was going to hate her for it.

"Go, Cory! Go, Cory! Go, Cory!" the kids were still chanting when Raven came back down the stairs.

Still beaming, Cory rushed up to her. "Listen to that!" he cried. "They think I'm the man!"

Raven nodded, suddenly feeling queasy, too—but her stomachache had nothing to do with bad seafood.

"I've got some bad news, sweetie," Raven said gently. "Mom and Dad have food poisoning. So, we have to cancel your party."

"You're canceling my party?" Cory howled in horror.

He'd said it loud enough for Billy Correll to hear—and it was exactly the opening the snotty kid had been waiting for. "Hey, Cory's party's a wipe!" he called to the group. "Who wants to go to *my* house?"

"They have a big-screen TV!" shouted Jaime, backing up his best friend.

A second later, the kids had left Cory's side of the room and moved over to Billy's. "Go, Billy! Go, Billy! Go, Billy!" they began to chant.

Cory looked completely crushed. "Great," he told Raven, "now I'm going to be a big joke. I knew I should have just gone to the movies."

Raven felt a stab of guilt. This whole party had been her idea, not Cory's—and now he was going to suffer for it.

"No," Raven said suddenly. She just could not let her brother down. "No, no, no, no, no. You know what? We can still have fun here, Cory. I'll tell you what. If we can't go to the zoo, then . . . uh . . . the zoo can come to us!"

"Really?" Cory asked, a ray of hope lighting up his face.

"Yes," Raven assured him.

"You can do that?" he asked.

Raven nodded, and a huge grin quickly replaced Cory's disappointed frown. "Hey, guys!" he yelled to all the kids. "My sister says the zoo's coming to us!"

Suddenly, the kids stopped cheering for Billy. "Go, Cory! Go, Cory! Go, Cory!" they chanted again as they left Billy in the dust and went back to Cory's side of the room. Cory clapped along as the kids surrounded him. Then the birthday boy began to dance.

Raven watched the whole scene with a tense smile. Okay, don't freak, she told herself. I can do this. I can. I've just got to get Eddie and

Chelsea over here. 'Cause, bottom line: 9-1-1 is *not* going to work in this situation. And I'm definitely going to need some—

HEEEEELP!

Chapter Four

"**O**kay, they ate all of the animal crackers—" said Raven, rushing into the kitchen with an empty bowl. "And now they want the real thing. So, did you find an animal guy that can come to the house?"

"Well, I tried," said Eddie. He'd just hung up from his third call. A thick phone book sat open on the kitchen counter. He pointed to the "Children's Party Entertainers" listings. "Sammy the Snake Man, Pythons on Parade, and the Lizards of Oz," he said. "They're all booked."

Just then, the back door swung open and Chelsea swept in with two big shopping bags in her hands.

"Oh, Chelsea, thank you so much," said Raven, rushing up to her. She'd called Chelsea earlier and told her to drop everything and bring over *any* party items she could get her hands on. "So how'd everything go?" she asked.

"Great!" Chelsea replied. "My mom had lots of party stuff. Hats and balloons and—oh, there's this 'Happy 50th Birthday' sign!"

"Great," said Raven. "Um, here's some scissors. Cut off forty years. Thank you!"

Then she turned back to Eddie and pulled the phone book closer. She turned the page and noticed a catchy name listed.

"Have you tried this guy named *Reptile Rick*?" she asked.

"Reptile Rick's coming to my party?"

Raven spun around to find her brother standing right behind her with an awestruck look on his face. She hadn't noticed him come in from the living room.

"Wow!" Cory went on. "He's even more fun than the zoo!" He ran to the kitchen door and shouted to the kids in the next room, "Hey, everybody, Reptile Rick's coming!"

There was a huge cheer, and Cory ran out of the kitchen, shutting the door behind him.

Dumbfounded, Raven just stared into space for a long moment. I am *so* sunk, she thought.

"Wow," said Chelsea, meeting Raven's horrified gaze.

"I know," said Raven.

"Going through your whole life with a first name like 'Reptile,'" Chelsea said, shaking her head in pity for the poor man.

Raven sighed. Chelsea was a good friend, but sometimes she was *so* in her own zone, Raven just didn't know what to do with her!

Well, I'm not giving up, Raven decided. She

marched right over to the kitchen phone, hit the speaker button, and dialed the Reptile guy's number.

After a few rings, she heard an answering machine click in. "G'day! Reptile Rick here," said a chipper Australian voice. "I'm on a bit of a walkabout. So leave me a message at the beep."

"Just forget it," said Eddie, hearing the machine's message. "I mean, he's probably already booked anyway."

But Raven picked up the receiver with determination. "You know what your problem is?" she told Eddie. "You just don't know how to handle these people. All right, listen to this."

At the sound of the beep on the other end of the line, Raven cleared her throat and began. "*G'day*, mate!" she exclaimed in her best imitation of an Australian accent. "This is

Ray-ven from Down Under. I need ya to come to a *par-tay* at 519 Miranda Place *lickety-splitsy*. All right, no worries, um, I'm in a bit of a . . . *wobbly. G'day!*"

Not bad, she thought to herself. Good thing she'd seen a few movies set in Australia. She turned to Eddie. "Whaddya think?"

Eddie just shook his head and told her, "I wouldn't bet my *wobbly* on it."

Later that morning, Raven stood in the middle of the living room, trying to keep Cory and his friends entertained. "Okay now," she said, standing over the redheaded Jaime, "with this hair and your complexion, I'd definitely say that you were a . . . let me see . . ." Raven checked his eye color. "Yes, you're an *autumn*."

She whipped out her color swatches and held a few different shades of fabric against the little boy's forehead. "So I'd stay away from the pinks and the peaches," she advised the con-fused little boy.

For the past hour and a half, Raven had led the boys in a sing-along, blown up balloons, fed them cake, and helped them play a game of pin-the-tail-on-the-donkey. She thought she'd run out of ideas—until she remembered how much fun doing people's colors had been at her second cousin's bridal shower.

"All right, now don't crowd around," said Raven. "I will do *everybody*. I'm just going to go check on the zoo. Aren't we having such fun!"

As Raven left the room, Cory glanced at his confused friends and shrugged. Obviously, they had *no idea* what his crazy sister was up to—and, frankly, neither did he!

Meanwhile, back in the kitchen, Raven was ready to tear her hair out. "So did Reptile Rick call back yet?" she asked in desperation.

"No, he didn't," said Eddie. "Rae, just face it, he's not coming."

Chelsea nodded in agreement. "Yeah, you're just going to have to tell Cory the truth, Rae," she said.

"And have him hate me?" said Raven. "Have him think I am the worst sister ever?"

"You're giving makeup advice to ten-year-old boys," Eddie pointed out. "I think that ship has sailed."

Just then, the door to the living room swung open, and Cory walked in with a look of disappointment on his face.

"Everyone wants to go home," he said sadly. "Is Reptile Rick coming or not?"

"Can I answer that?" an Australian voice called through the kitchen's back door.

"Reptile Rick!" squealed Cory, racing over to greet him.

Through the door strode a tall, blond man

wearing khaki pants, a khaki vest, black leather boots, and an authentic Australian bush hat. In one hand, Reptile Rick held a large cage. And in his other hand was a leash—with a big, furry *pig* at the end of it!

"That's right, mate. I'm Reptile Rick," the man told Cory. "And you must be the birthday boy."

With a big smile, Rick placed a smaller version of his bush hat on Cory's head. Cory's eyes widened with pure delight. "Everyone!" he shouted, running into the living room. "Everyone, Reptile Rick is here!"

All the kids cheered.

"You must be Raven," said Reptile Rick, walking up to her. His furry pig waddled along right beside him.

"Yeah," said Raven, eyeing the pig worriedly. To her it looked awfully big. And awfully . . . piggy.

"Take that," Rick said, handing her its leash.

"That's—oh! Oh, okay, Rick," said Raven, startled by the size of the animal. "Well, this isn't exactly the *lizard* that I ordered. Because I thought your name was *Reptile* Rick, not *Big-Pig-In-My-Kitchen* Rick!"

"Easy, Sheila," said Rick. "I got all the reptiles you want out in the truck."

He set the cage down on the counter. Chelsea glanced inside.

"Personally," she told Rick, "I don't really think animals should be kept in cages."

"Oh, yeah?" he said. "Neither do I. Let's let it out, shall we?"

But just as Rick was reaching to unlatch the reptile's cage, Eddie lunged in to stop him. "Nooooooo!" he cried in terror. Embarrassed, he quickly added, "I mean, uh, it might scare the *kids*."

"R-i-i-i-ight," said Rick, not believing him for a second.

Chelsea walked over to the pig and crouched down. "So, is this little guy part of your act?" she asked, petting the pig's long, black fur.

"Oh, no," said Rick. "This is Fanny, my potbellied pig. Isn't she a beaut? Couldn't leave her in the truck," he added. "Last time I did, she squealed on me." Rick laughed. "*Squealed on me,*" he repeated, waiting for Chelsea to laugh, too. But she just stared at him blankly.

"You don't get it," said Rick with a sigh. "Anyway," he continued, looking at Raven, "you got anything to eat? I just did four shows with no lunch. I'm *starving.*"

Just then, Raven heard her mother calling from upstairs, "Rae!"

"Oh, that's my mom," Raven told Rick. "So, you go get whatever you need." She pointed to the refrigerator and cupboards. "Just search around." Raven turned to Chelsea. "And I need *you* to go check on the children while I go check on my mom."

Chelsea nodded and headed out to the living room.

Then, Raven turned to Eddie. "And *you* need to keep whatever's in there—in there." She pointed to the mysterious reptile cage. "Don't let it come out."

Eddie nodded like his life depended on it—and he was honestly afraid it *did*.

"And *you*," she said to the big drooling pig, "okay, *you* need a tissue!"

Chapter Five

"**S**o are you guys feeling okay?" Raven asked her parents when she got to their bedroom. Her mother and father were still sick in bed, but she could see they looked worried.

"What's all that noise downstairs?" asked Mrs. Baxter.

"Oh, that," said Raven. "That's just Cory and his friends. 'Cause, Mama, I really didn't have the heart to cancel his party, so I'm just doing a little something for him downstairs. Nothing big." Just a little entertainment involving a few reptiles and a wacky Australian man with a potbellied pig on a leash, Raven added silently to herself.

Her mother and father nodded between

groans. "Why don't you let them watch some videos or something," suggested Raven's father.

"The last thing we need is a zoo down there," Raven's mother warned.

"*Interesting* choice of words," Raven replied, hoping her mother hadn't suddenly become psychic, too!

Leaving their bedroom, Raven raced back down the stairs. Okay, she thought, now that Rick is here, we can finally get this reptile party started! She strode into the kitchen—and stopped dead.

Reptile Rick was sitting at the counter with all of his reptile cages stacked around him. But the iguanas, frogs, chameleons, and snakes weren't the problem. The problem was Rick's lunch. The man was finishing up the leftover linguine and clams her parents had brought home from the seafood restaurant the night before. Raven's mother had warned her to throw out the container, but with all the craziness, she'd forgotten!

"Hey, no, Rick!" Raven cried, rushing up to him. "You're not supposed to eat that. My parents got *sick* from that!"

But Reptile Rick just laughed and continued to wolf down the cold linguine. "Don't worry about me, Sheila," he said. "I've eaten *snakes*. I've eaten *lizards*. I've eaten *rats* on a stick in the noonday sun. Old Reptile Rick's got a cast-iron stomach."

Just to make his point, he patted his stomach—which suddenly made a very unsettling sound. This was followed by a very unsettling expression on Rick's face. It was the exact same seasick look Raven had seen on her mother and father!

"Waltzing Matilda!" cried Rick. "Where's the dunny?"

"The whaty?" asked Raven. She'd learned plenty of Australian slang watching movies, but that one had never come up.

"The dunny," he repeated. "The loo!"

"The who?" asked Raven.

"The . . . oh, never mind," said Rick and he tore out the kitchen door, followed by Fanny, his faithful pig.

"Hey, Reptile? Can't you get sick in front of the kids?" called Raven, more than a little desperate. "I mean, they'd *love* that."

Fifteen minutes later, Raven and Chelsea stood in the kitchen, crossing their fingers for good luck, as Eddie burst into the living room.

"Okay, are you all ready for Reptile Rick?" Eddie shouted to the room full of kids.

"Yeah!" cheered the birthday guests.

"Well, uh, he's throwin' up," Eddie mumbled. "So he-e-e-re's Reptile *Raven*!"

Hearing her cue, Raven took a deep breath and made her big entrance. She'd borrowed Rick's bush hat and khaki vest. And she'd borrowed one of his reptiles, too—a huge green iguana.

"Voilà!" cried Raven. "Iguana!"

For a minute, she just stood there with a tight grin on her face and the iguana in her arms.

"*Do* something with it!" shouted the snotty Billy.

Trying not to panic, Raven glanced over at Eddie—who immediately began to beatbox, "boom-shh-shh-shh, boom-shh-shh-shh-shh, boom-shh-shh-shh, boom-shh-shh-shh-shh . . ."

Okay, Raven told herself, time to get jiggy with the reptile.

"Dan-cing ig-uana," she rapped, "dan-cing ig-uana, dan-cing ig-uana, dan-cing ig-uana . . ." She moved across the room, waving the creepy thing back and forth.

"Oh!" she cried, looking down at Rick's vest, which was suddenly wet. Time to change the lyric, she thought. "Pee-ing ig-uana," she revised, "pee-ing ig-uana, pee-ing ig-uana, pee-ing ig-uana . . ."

"This party stinks," complained Billy.

"Where are the snakes?" yelled Jaime.

Raven turned to the kids. "*Snaykes?*" she loudly repeated, using her fake Australian accent. "Ya want snaykes? Well, I'll get ya snaykes."

She started toward the kitchen, when Cory tugged her sleeve and whispered, "But you hate snakes."

"Are ya kidding me," she declared confidently. "Rayptile Rayven laaahves snaykes!"

The kids cheered.

"Oh, I hate snakes," Raven whimpered to herself as she dashed through the kitchen door and closed it behind her.

"But not as much as I hate frogs!" she cried when she saw the state of her kitchen. The entire room was covered in them. And Raven knew exactly why. She glared at her anti-caged-animal friend.

"Actually, they're South American bull-frogs," Chelsea explained. "And they hate being in cages. They were talking to me." She leaned down to peer at one of their little faces. "'Unlockit, unlockit,'" she repeated, imitating a froggy voice.

Raven sighed in total frustration. My girl has obviously returned to that very special *zone* of hers, she thought. What Raven wanted to know was why Eddie hadn't stopped her. Come to think of it, where *was* Eddie? She looked around—and found him standing on a chair. One of the bullfrogs leaped at him and he squealed in horror.

"What?" Eddie said when he saw Raven's

look. "I just don't want to step on them. They're *endangered*, you know."

Suddenly, Raven felt a vision coming on. Eyes wide, she watched and waited, desperately hoping her next glimpse of the future would show her some way *out* of this mess . . .

Through her eye
The vision runs
Flash of future
Here it comes—

I see my parents' bedroom. They're still sick in bed. That can only mean one thing: this vision is going to happen TODAY.

My mother is tossing and turning. "What is all that noise down there?" she says.

"I don't know," my father tells her. Now he's throwing off the covers and heading for the bedroom door. "But I'm going to find out . . ."

The second she came out of her vision, Raven freaked. "Oh, my goodness!" she cried. If my father comes downstairs and finds out his house has been turned into Animal Planet, Raven thought, I am definitely going to end up on Grounded Planet—for a *long* time.

"My dad's going to come downstairs!" Raven warned her friends. "We've got to get rid of these frogs!"

"Okay, okay, I've got it covered," said Eddie, still on his chair. "Fellas, back in the cage!" he coaxed, snapping his fingers as if they were tiny, web-footed Chihuahuas.

"Eddie!" cried Raven. "Stop snappin' and start grabbin'. Come on!"

All three friends raced around the room, picking up the hopping bullfrogs. They hid them in cabinets, pots, cookie jars—anything that seemed handy.

"Rae," came a deep voice from upstairs, "you down there?"

Oh, snap! thought Raven. It was her father. He was coming downstairs—just like she'd seen in her vision! With no time left, Raven, Chelsea, and Eddie began to stuff the remaining frogs into their pockets and down their shirts and pants.

A minute later, Mr. Baxter walked into the kitchen. Raven froze. So did Eddie and Chelsea. All three gave Raven's father innocent smiles.

"Just came down to see what all this noise was about," said Mr. Baxter.

"Noise? Oh, Dad," said Raven, "I'm sorry. I'll be sure to keep it—" Suddenly, she twitched and squealed as one of the frogs leaped inside her shirt. "—DOWN! How are you doing, you know, are you feeling okay?" she finished.

"Yeah," said Mr. Baxter, opening the fridge. "Well, maybe a little ginger ale will help."

Raven's dad grabbed the plastic bottle of soda. Just as he closed the door and turned around, a bullfrog hopped from the top of the fridge onto Mr. Baxter's head.

Raven held her breath.

"I don't know," Mr. Baxter told Raven, standing there in his bathrobe, not even noticing that a South American bullfrog was now sitting on top of his bald head. "My head's starting to feel a little clammy. Do I look okay?"

Raven swallowed nervously. Sure, dad, she almost said. As a lily pad, you look slammin'!

"Dad, you look good," she told him. "But, uh, I think I just need to, uh, check your fever. So let me see your head." Raven rushed over and put her palm against her father's brow. "Right. Oh, what's that!" she suddenly cried, pointing to the other side of the room.

"What?" asked her father, turning to look.

In a flash, Raven snatched the frog off her dad's head and threw it to Eddie, who stuffed it down his shirt.

"Nothing, nothing," said Raven when her father turned back. "You're okay."

Mr. Baxter nodded and crossed back toward the stairs. But when he noticed Chelsea and Eddie spastically twitching and squirming, he stopped and stared at them.

"Is everything okay?" he asked.

"We're just . . . just . . ." stammered Eddie.

"Feeling the groove, Mr. Baxter!" Chelsea cried. "Whoo, yeah! Can you feel it?"

Suddenly, all three kids started dancing—without music. Mr. Baxter stared at them in bewilderment. He was already starting to feel dizzy again, and he wasn't sure what to make of their strange behavior.

"Well, could you kids not move so much?"

he asked. "Because you're making me want to . . . oh, I gotta go!"

And before you can say "linguine with clams," Raven's dad was outie!

Chapter Six

"**O**kay, everybody's ready for the snakes," Cory told Raven, racing into the kitchen. "This is going to be *so* cool!"

Raven grinned. Not just because she, Eddie, and Chelsea had managed to wrangle all the bullfrogs back into their cage—without her father catching on—but because her little brother seemed so excited.

"Anything to make you happy," Raven told Cory.

Cory gave his sister a thumbs-up, she gave him one in return, and Cory headed back to the living room.

As the kids watched, the door to the kitchen flew open. Raven stepped out and struck a dramatic supermodel pose. She was still wear-ing the Australian bush hat and vest, but now, wrapped like a hot new fashion accessory, a huge boa constrictor dangled from her neck.

As Raven walked across the room like a runway model, Chelsea began to describe her "look." "Raven Baxter is modeling this year's newest fall fashion," Chelsea declared. "Her new line of boas!"

Raven stopped, smiled tightly, and turned like a supermodel. She still *hated* snakes—but for Cory's sake, she was doing her best to think of the disgusting thing as some sort of scaly, gotta-have-it scarf.

"Yes, it's what every girl should have around her neck this year," Chelsea continued. "And guys, with the holiday seasons coming up, what better way to say, 'I love you,' than a new boa?"

Snakeskin boots, Raven thought as she

strutted and spun, forcing her mind to picture the sort of snake that *wasn't* scary. *Snakeskin belts. Snakeskin handbags . . .*

Then she caught site of the creature's snake-skin *head* hanging only a few inches from her own—and she started to freak. Quickly, she headed back toward the kitchen door.

"Okay!" said Chelsea, seeing Raven's rush to exit. Immediately, she speeded up her own delivery. "Available in spots and solids, up to twenty-five feet long. Mice not included. Thank you so much. Buh-bye!"

Raven raced into the kitchen. "Get it off! Get it off!" she squealed.

But when she saw her little brother burst through the door, she froze. Instantly, the calm, cool snake-wrangler mask went back on. "Hey, Cory," said Raven cheerfully. "Pretty cool snake, huh? Can't hate me for that."

"They're *laughing* out there," Cory

complained. "Reptile Rick doesn't *model* snakes, he *wrestles* them."

"He does?" Raven asked weakly, thinking, wrestle . . . snakes . . . me?

You're mental! Raven wanted to scream, but she didn't. Instead, she told Cory to go back to the living room and wait for her next "show."

Then she looked helplessly at her best friends. If ever she needed Eddie and Chelsea to come up with a great idea—or even a *not-so-great one*—it was right now.

The lights went out in the living room. All was dark. A shiver of excitement went through the birthday crowd.

Eddie began to bang on a pair of bongo drums. On the front stairs, Chelsea held two flashlights under her chin to make her face appear as if it were floating in the air.

"And now," she announced, "for the first

time in the United States, Reptile Raven will attempt to wrestle one of the world's deadliest reptiles—the man-eating anaconda!"

Eddie banged his bongos like crazy. Reptile Raven raced down the stairs, holding a big cardboard box.

Chelsea shone the flashlights on Raven so the crowd could see. Raven was still wearing Rick's khaki vest, but she'd taken off the Australian bush hat. She was ready to wrestle!

"All right," said Raven in her Australian accent, holding the box up and moving it around. "It's a big one. He's in the box. He might bite off me arm or maybe me leg. Ya never know. A chance you have to take with . . . *anaconda*!"

Slowly, Reptile Raven opened the box. Then she screamed and lunged behind the couch.

The kids were awestruck. Their eyes stayed glued to Cory's big sister as she rose up again, this time with a giant snake wrapped around her neck!

Flipping one way, then another, Raven wrestled the snake. Grunting and yelling, she popped up and down behind the couch until she finally stood up and pointed to the floor.

"I think it's dead . . . Oh, crikey, it's got me hand!" she shouted. "It's all right, I think I've got it. No, wait . . . aaahhh!"

Suddenly, the snake pulled her back behind the couch. She leaped up and began swinging it above her head. Then she dove down again.

The kids were loving it—until Jaime flipped the light switch. All the kids raced forward to peer behind the couch. They were eager to see the dead snake.

But when they looked, they saw it wasn't dead. It wasn't a snake, either.

"It's just a stupid stuffed animal!" cried Billy.

Caught in the fake-out act, Raven tried to cover. "It is?" she said, acting surprised. "I guess that's why it hasn't been eating the mice."

Totally busted, Raven thought. She stood up with her "snake," a funny-looking stuffed animal her mother had won at a school carnival.

"This party reeks," complained Jaime.

"I'm going home," said Billy. "Who wants to come?"

"I do," said Cory.

Raven was devastated. Her little brother was no longer looking at her with joy—he was glaring at her with hurt, disappointment, and anger.

All the kids filed out of the house. Cory was the last to go. "Cory, wait!" cried Raven. She just couldn't let him leave like this.

Standing by the front door, Cory turned

and glared at Raven again. Then he took off his bush hat and threw it to the floor.

Raven gasped. This is it, she thought in horror. Her awful vision was coming true!

"This is the worst party," Cory began, "and you're the—"

"Stop!" cried Raven, before he could say another word. "Okay, I know what you're going to say. Come here." Raven shut the front door and took her brother's hand. She led him to the living room sofa and sat down.

"Listen," she continued, "I know you want to say I was the worst sister ever and you hate me, and I don't blame you. I ruined your birthday, I always argue with you, and I know I'm not the nicest sister. But I just don't want us to stop talking, you know. I want us to always be friends. And even when we fight, I still love you."

Before Cory could answer, they were interrupted. Jaime opened the front door and stuck his head inside.

"Hey, Baxter," he called excitedly, "you've got to come see this!"

Curious, both Cory and Raven walked out the front door. On the edge of the porch, all the kids had crowded around a big blanket. Reptile Rick was sitting on it next to Fanny—and her new litter of potbellied piglets!

"Aw, see that? See his little nose?" Rick told the captivated kids, pointing to the piglet's pink nostrils. "It's sniffin' for milk."

Reptile Rick noticed Raven and Cory, and he waved them over with a grin. "Come over here, birthday boy. Take a closer look. Fanny just had her babies."

Cory sat down next to Billy, who was holding one of the piglets. "This is so cool,"

Billy told Cory as he pet the piglet's soft head.

Jaime nodded in agreement. He patted Cory on the back. "Great party, Baxter!"

"Really?" asked Cory, relieved.

All the kids nodded, smiling, and Cory gave his sister a grateful look.

"So, you don't hate me?" whispered Raven.

"Well, I kind of thought I did," he admitted. "But how many sisters would do all this for their little brother?"

"So, we're okay?" she asked.

"No," he said. Then he smiled. "We're *great.*"

"Well, I'm all packed up," said Reptile Rick, standing in the Baxters' kitchen an hour later. He smiled down at Cory. "I'm glad your party worked out for ya, little fella. Fanny's going to remember it, that's for sure!"

Raven grinned at the snake man. I am *so* good, she thought. Not only did I give my little brother the best birthday party he ever had, I managed to keep my parents from noticing an entire zoo of reptiles running wild in their house.

Go, Raven! Go, Raven! Go, Raven! she chanted to herself.

"Now," said Reptile Rick, "all I need is my snake back."

"It's in the cage," said Cory, pointing.

"What? *That?*" said Rick, glancing into the cage. "Aw, nah, that's the *baby*. I'm looking for its mama."

Raven nearly choked. "The *mama*?" she and Cory squeaked together.

At that very same moment, Raven's own mama—and her daddy, too—were gaping in horror at a twenty-foot python slithering up their bedcovers.

"Raven!"

In the kitchen, Raven heard her parents' ter-rified voices and squeezed her eyes shut. Well, she thought, I *almost* got away with it.

Gaze into the future and take a sneak peek at the next *That's So Raven* story. . . .

Adapted by Jasmine Jones
Based on the series created by
Michael Poryes
Susan Sherman
Based on the teleplay written by
Laura Perkins-Brittain & Carla Banks Waddles

"**N**o, Tanya, there's no need to worry," Raven's father, Victor Baxter, said into the phone.

Sitting at the breakfast table, Raven could

hear her mother's voice blaring from the receiver, even though her father was on the other side of the kitchen. Raven's mom was visiting her parents, which meant that her dad was in charge at home. Mrs. Baxter was usually cool as a cucumber, Raven noted, but she always went halfway to mental when she left home, as if she thought the family might fall apart while she was away, or something.

"Everything is running smoothly here," Mr. Baxter assured his wife. Just then, the toaster popped up. Raven's dad held out a plate and caught the toast as it sailed through the air. Now that *was* smooth, Raven thought.

"Rae, will you tell your mother everything's fine?" Mr. Baxter asked, handing her the cordless and setting the plate of toast down in front of her.

"Hi, Mom," Raven said into the phone. "We haven't eaten for days, your plants are dead, and I'm dropping out of school. Love ya. Bye." She absently brushed a piece of lint from her black sweater as she handed the phone back to her dad, who looked horrified. Oops, Raven thought. I forgot that Mom has zero sense of humor when it comes to being away from home.

"It was a *joke*," Mr. Baxter insisted into the receiver as he placed a sandwich stuffed with gourmet meats and cheeses in Cory's lunch box. Raven's dad was a chef, which meant Raven and her brother Cory had the best lunches in the world. Of course, it made the cafeteria food, when they had to eat it, seem a whole lot worse.

"No, no, Cory's a big boy," Mr. Baxter told his wife. "I let him pick out his clothes for school."

Just then, Cory walked into the kitchen wearing flip-flops, Hawaiian shorts, a tank top . . . and a giant inflatable duck-shaped inner tube around his waist.

Uh-uh, Raven thought, now I know that isn't *my* brother dressed like some kind of Orange Bowl float. Wherever Raven got her fashion sense from, the genes had definitely not been passed on to Cory. What he had was more like fashion *non*sense.

"Uh, Cory can't come to the phone right now," Mr. Baxter said quickly, eyeing Cory's outfit, "but I'll send him your love. Tell your folks I said hello. Bye-bye." Mr. Baxter hung up the phone and faced his son. "Cory, what do you have on?" he asked.

"I'm making a statement," Cory announced. "This says, 'Hi, I'm Cory. Wanna float my boat?'"

"Oh, really?" Raven said. "'Cause I'm hearing, 'Hi, I'm Cory. Wanna beat me up?'"

"Cory, go upstairs and put on something

that doesn't quack," Mr. Baxter commanded, folding his arms across his chest.

Raven stood up and took her plate of untouched toast to the kitchen counter.

"Come on, Rae," her dad griped, "you've got to eat something before you go to school."

"I'm too nervous, Dad," Raven insisted. "They're announcing who's getting the parts in *The Wizard of Oz* today." Okay, so I haven't had a psychic vision about it, Raven thought, but I have a feeling that there will be a bunch of singing munchkins in my future.

"Let me guess," Mr. Baxter said, grabbing Raven's long, black braids and giving them a gentle tug. "You're going up for the role of Dorothy."

"Yes, Dad, but I already made my costume. Say good-bye to Dorothy's frumpy blue little farm dress," Raven said, holding up her latest fashion creation, a blue-and-white checked miniskirt trimmed in sparkly tulle. "And say hello to her new mini."

Mr. Baxter frowned. "If Dorothy is still skipping down the yellow brick road, that hemline better come *way* down."

Raven looked at the skirt again. Okay, Dad does have a point, she had to admit.

"Come on, Cory!" Mr. Baxter hollered up the stairs. He turned to Raven. "I've got to get to the restaurant early today," he said. "The new owner, Mr. Briggs? Two words: not nice."

Cory appeared at the bottom of the stairs, dressed more or less as a normal human being in jeans and a striped shirt. "I'm ready now," he said, glaring at his father. "My creativity has been squashed, but I am ready."

"Well, good luck with the new boss," Raven told her dad.

"Oh, come on, Rae, I get along with everybody." Mr. Baxter waved his hand dismissively and handed Cory his lunch box. "That restaurant's had lots of owners, but only one chef . . . your old man. Now please, please . . ." He grabbed a bright green apple out of the fruit bowl and handed it to Raven. "Eat something," he told her. He kissed Raven on the forehead, then followed Cory out the back door.

"Okay, okay," Raven promised, taking the apple.

Suddenly, the world began to spin. The kitchen went hazy, and Raven felt as though time had frozen. . . .

Through her eye
The vision runs
Flash of future
Here it comes—

Where am I? It looks like Augustine's, the restaurant where Dad works.

Hey, look, there's Dad! He looks so much taller in his chef's hat. But who's that weasely little guy with the sour face? He looks as pinched as a dried-up old apple.

"I've heard enough out of you, Baxter!" the man says. "You're fired!"

Oh, no. I just realized who that man is. It's Mr. Briggs, Dad's new boss.

And Dad is about to get terminated!

Raven came out of her vision and swallowed hard. That vision was no joke. She had to warn her dad!

FIRST TIME ON DVD AND VIDEO

Sassy, Stylish and Psychic!

FEATURES NEVER-BEFORE-SEEN EPISODE

that's so raven

Supernaturally Stylish

COMING DECEMBER 7

Disney CHANNEL

Walt Disney HOME ENTERTAINMENT

Get Cheetah Power!

the Cheetah Girls

Includes An
Alternate Ending
& Exclusive
Behind-The-Scenes
Look

133

Now on DVD and Video

Groove to the Sound of all your favorite shows

Disney Channel Soundtrack Series

Disney's
Kim Possible
TV Soundtrack

The Cheetah Girls
TV Soundtrack

Lizzie McGuire
TV Soundtrack

Pixel Perfect
Soundtrack

Also, look for...

- ***The Proud Family* TV Series Soundtrack**
- ***That's So Raven* TV Series Soundtrack**

Collect them all!

Wake up.

Go to school.

Save the world.

Will   Irma   Taranee   Cornelia   Hay Lin

The magic of friendship

The new book series · Make some powerful friends at www.clubwitch.com